For Megan, Charlie,
Lucy and George –
and thank you to Grandpa.

This paperback edition first published in 2010
by Andersen Press Ltd.
First published in Great Britain in 2010 by Andersen Press Ltd.,
20 Vauxhall Bridge Road, London SW1V 2SA.
Published in Australia by Random House Australia Pty.,
Level 3, 100 Pacific Highway, North Sydney, NSW 2060.
Copyright © Jo Hodgkinson, 2010
The rights of Jo Hodgkinson to be identified
as the author and illustrator of this work
have been asserted by her in accordance with
the Copyright, Designs and Patents Act, 1988.
All rights reserved.
Colour separated in Switzerland by Photolitho AG, Zürich.
Printed and bound in Singapore by Tien Wah Press.

10   9   8   7   6   5   4   3   2

British Library Cataloguing in Publication Data available.
ISBN 978 1 84939 076 7
This book has been printed on acid-free paper

A sign stopped four friends in their tracks.
The news sent shivers down their backs.

A small red bird who'd seen it too
Flew down to get a better view.
He quietly said, "I'd like a go
To try and win this Talent Show."

The four friends laughed. "Don't be absurd!
You're much too small. You're just a bird."

With that the friends went on their way
To practise for this special day.

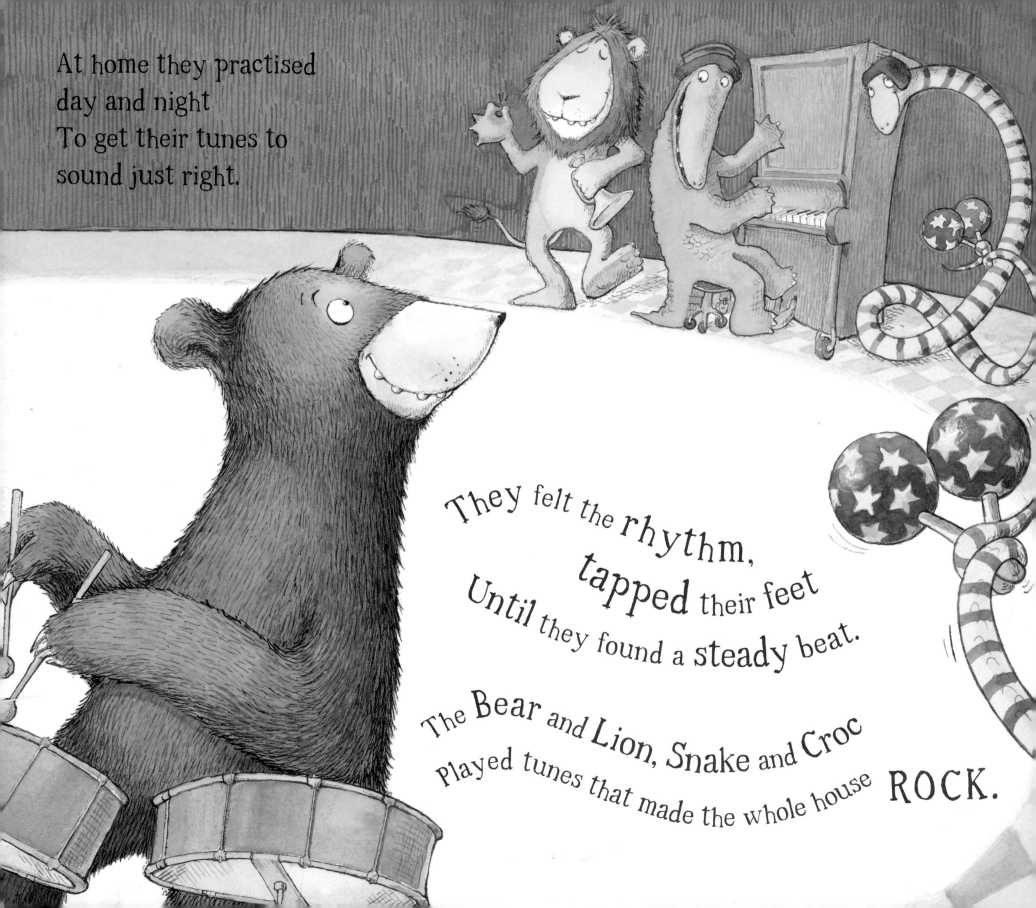

At home they practised
day and night
To get their tunes to
sound just right.

They felt the rhythm,
tapped their feet
Until they found a steady beat.

The Bear and Lion, Snake and Croc
Played tunes that made the whole house ROCK.

This band could play. This band could move.

This band had really found their groove.

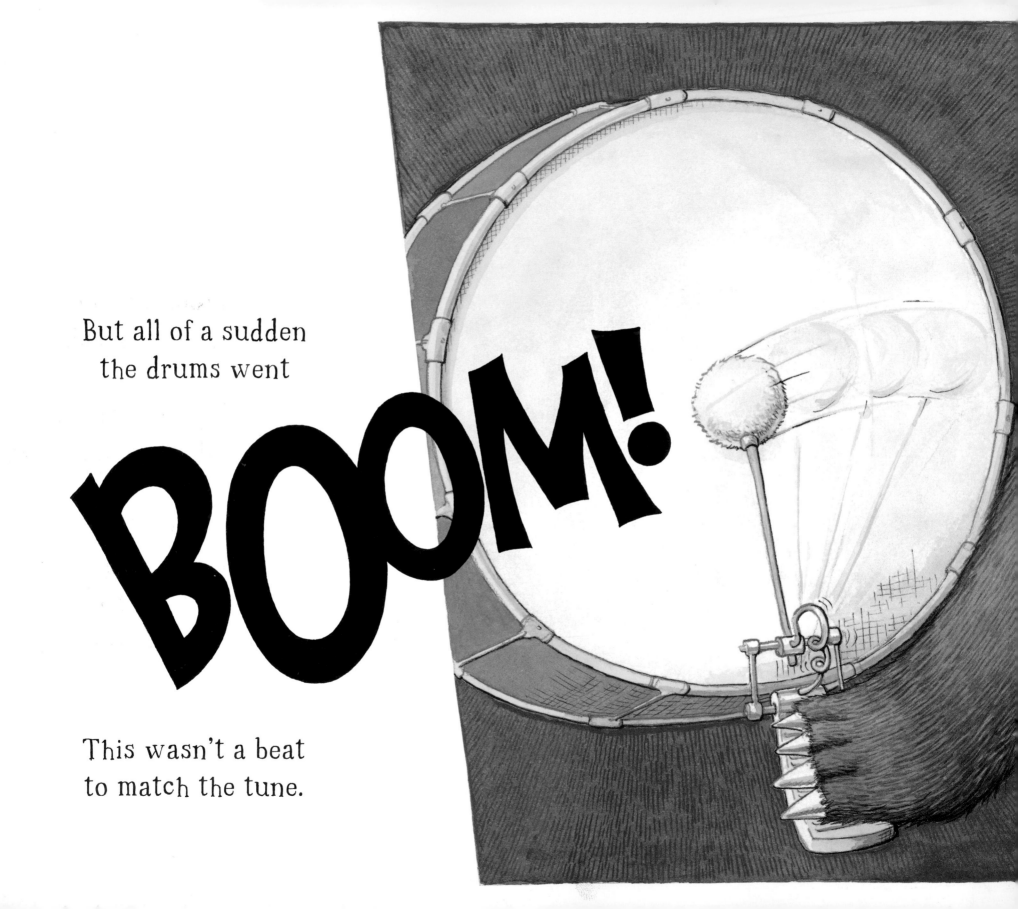

But all of a sudden
the drums went

BOOM!

This wasn't a beat
to match the tune.

Bear stood up and scratched his head.

Looked quite serious, sighed and said,

"If we want to win this thing, One of the band will have to sing."

So everybody took a turn
To sing a song that they had learnt.

But the only sounds that
they could make
Were GRR, SNAP, GROWL
and HISS of snake.

This came as quite a big surprise.
"I know," said Croc, "let's advertise!"
They hung a sign up in the tree,
So singers passing by might see.

SINGER
WANTED

auditions
today

This way

Well not much time
had passed before
They heard a knock
at their front door.

As Bear looked out
onto the street,
He heard a voice
down by his feet.

"I saw the sign so down I flew.
I've come to have an interview."

Bear growled,
"There's nothing left to say.
You're much too small.
Now GO AWAY!"

Singers came from all around.

But no one had that missing sound. With no hope left, what would they do?
The band sat down to think things through. When suddenly they got a shock . . .

A loud, resounding KNOCK KNOCK KNOCK!

They looked and
saw an eerie sight.
A stranger standing
in the night.

His coat was long,
his glasses black,
And on his head
he wore a hat.

He said, "I've come
to help you win
This Talent Show.
Can I come in?"

He sang the most amazing songs.

The band began to play along.

They knew this was
the missing sound.

At last their singer
had been found.

But as he sang and danced around

The stranger's coat fell to the ground.

And in their presence now they saw
The bird they'd laughed at twice before.

"Red-Bird, will you forgive us, please?
We realize we were wrong to tease."

Bird said, "You really were unwise
To simply judge me by my size.
But now I see you understand
And I'd be glad to join your band."

FACT 1.

Birds are very good at singing.

The Bird

The next day at the Talent Show,
the five were waiting for their go.

But as they stepped into the light . . .
The small red bird was filled with fright.

He felt so small and all alone.
He thought about his tree-top home.
He wished that he could fly away.
But then his friends began to play . . .

The rhythm started in his feet

And travelled quickly to his beak.

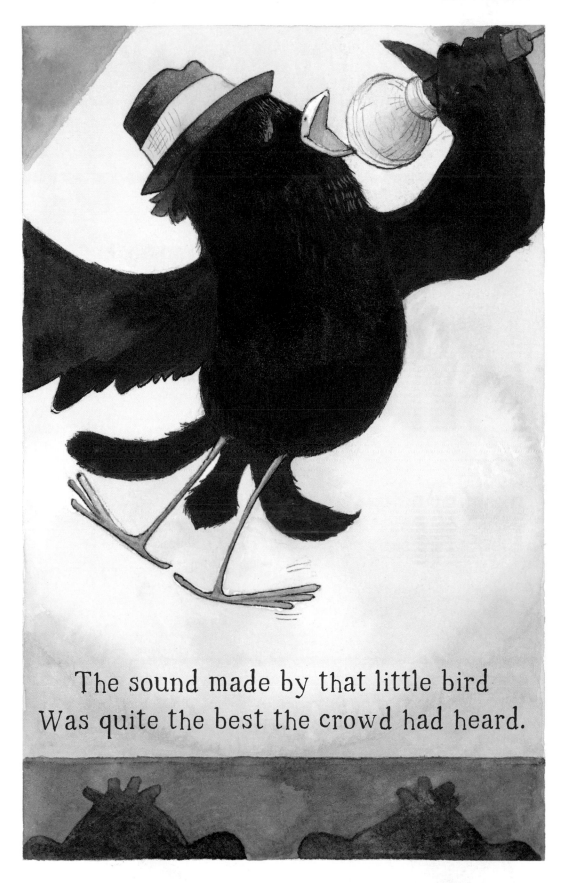

The sound made by that little bird
Was quite the best the crowd had heard.

The crowd got up, they danced and swayed
To every tune the great band played.

And as the crowd began to cheer
Bird saw he had no need to fear.
The judges gave the band the prize.
They judged on talent, not on size.

If you liked this book, you'll love these too:

9781849390149

9781849392242

9781849390736

9781849390576

9781849390293

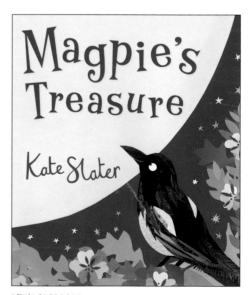

9781849390088